I'm Reading About

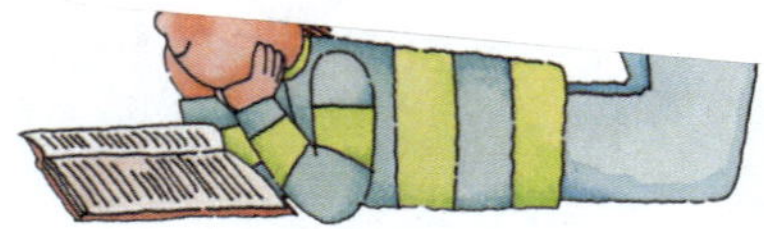

WASHINGTON, D.C.

GALLOPADE

by Carole Marsh

Printed and Manufactured in Peachtree City, GA., USA www.gallopade.com

Book design: Susan Van Denhende

Editor: Janice Baker

Washington, D.C.,
is a great place to visit!

What is so special about
Washington, D.C.?

Let’s read about it and see!

U.S. CAPITAL

Washington, D.C., is the capital of the United States.
It is the home of America's government.
America's laws are made here!

Washington, D.C., is named after George Washington.
He was the first President of the United States.

Nation's Capital

LOCATION

Washington, D.C., is in the eastern United States.
It is located along the Potomac River
between Maryland and Virginia.

Washington, D.C., is not a state.
It is a “federal district.”
The letters “D.C.” stand for “District of Columbia.”

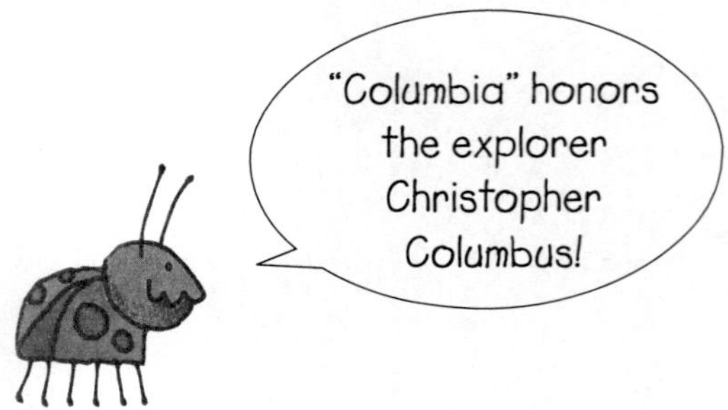

Washington, D.C.

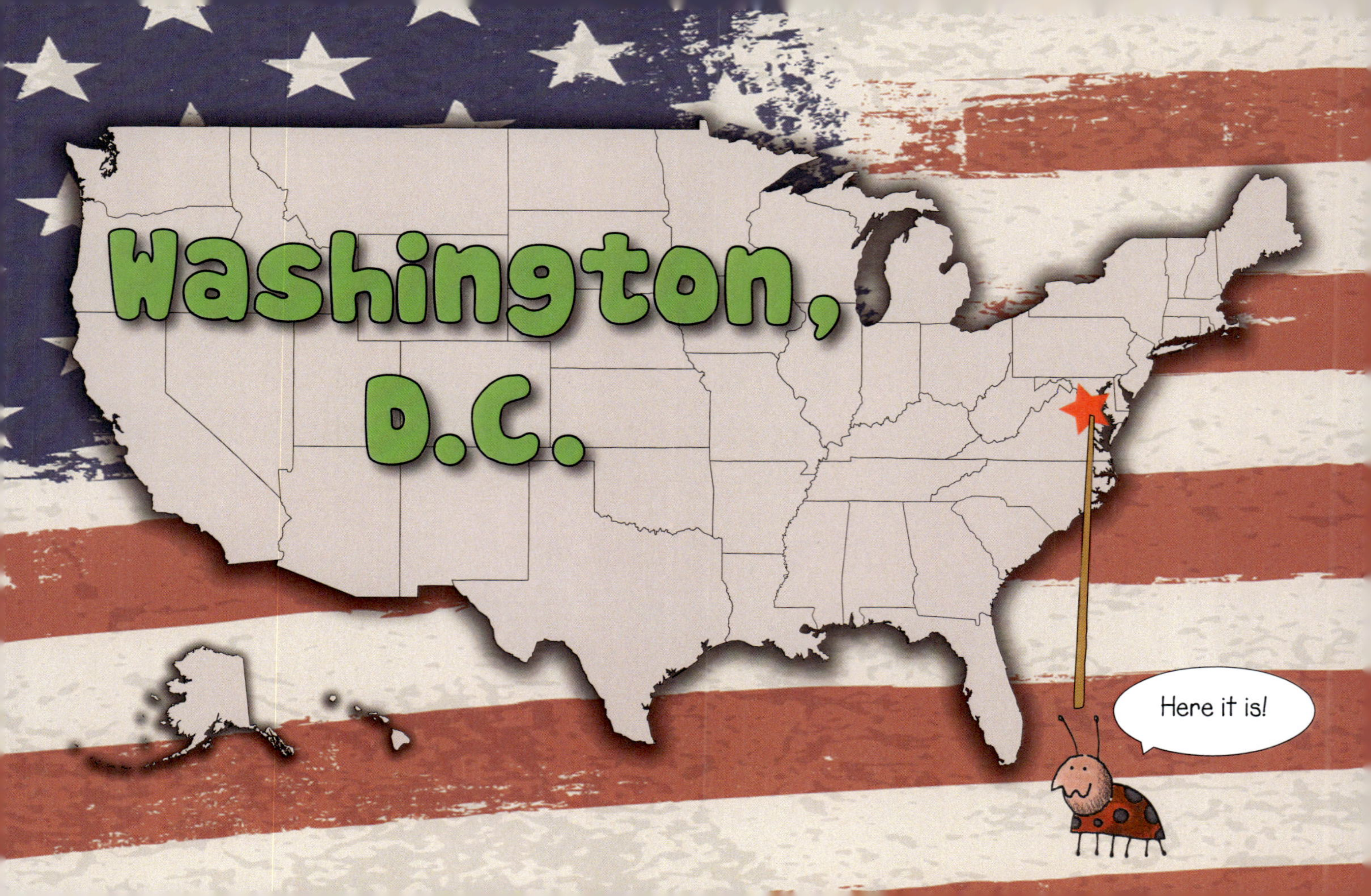

HISTORY

Before Washington, D.C., became the U.S. capital,
Congress met in several different cities.
They needed a permanent location!

In 1790, Congress passed a law.
It allowed President Washington to choose
the spot for the nation's capital
along the Potomac River.

Pierre L'Enfant was
the man
who carefully drew
the city's plan!

City Plan

PLAN of the City of WASHINGTON.
George Town
Tiber Creek
POTOMAK RIVER
EASTERN BRANCH
Lat: Capitol 38: 53, N.
Long: 0: 0.

U.S. CAPITAL

I am the U.S. Capitol building!
I am home to the U.S. Congress.
America's laws are made here!

A few fun facts about me:

- I have over 500 rooms and more than 600 windows.
- My dome is made of about 9 million pounds of cast iron.
- The statue on my dome is called the Statue of Freedom!

U.S. Capitol

WHITE HOUSE

I am the White House.
The President of the United States
lives and works here.
His office is called the "Oval Office."

The President's family lives here too.
They bring their dogs, cats, and other pets.
I don't mind!
I like to make the First Family
feel right at home!

The White House has
132 rooms, 35 bathrooms, and 6 levels!

White House

MONUMENT

I am the Washington Monument.
I am an obelisk.
I was built to honor President George Washington.

Did you know?

- I have a stairway of 897 steps.
- Fifty American flags circle my base.
- I am the tallest building in Washington, D.C.
- Lightning rods at the top protect me from lightning strikes!

Washington Monument

MEMORIAL

I am the Jefferson Memorial.
I was built to honor President Thomas Jefferson.
He was the third President of the United States.

A statue of President Jefferson
stands inside my walls.
It is 19 feet tall
and weighs 10,000 pounds!

The marble in the memorial's
steps came from four states:
Georgia, Missouri,
Tennessee, and Vermont.

Jefferson Memorial

Lincoln Memorial

MEMORIAL

I am the Lincoln Memorial.
I was built to honor President Abraham Lincoln.

Abraham Lincoln was the
16th President of the United States.
He guided the United States through the Civil War.

Inside, you can see a marble statue of President Lincoln.
Sculptors took four years to complete it!

Martin Luther King, Jr. Memorial

MEMORIAL

I am the Martin Luther King, Jr. Memorial.
I was built to honor Dr. Martin Luther King, Jr.

Dr. King was a civil rights leader.
He fought for equal rights for African Americans.
His message was:

Freedom **Justice** **Equality**

The memorial statue
is 30 feet tall!

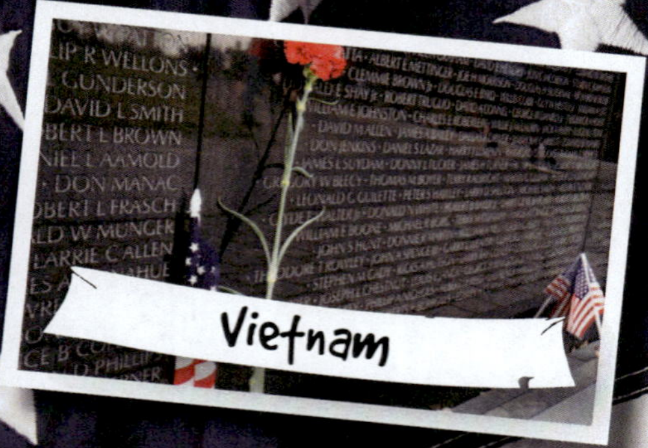

War Memorials

MEMORIALS

Washington, D.C., is home to many war memorials.
They honor men and women
who died serving our country.

These war memorials include:

- World War II Memorial
- Marine Corps War Memorial
- Korean War Veterans Memorial
- Vietnam Veterans Memorial

National Archives

ARCHIVES

I am known as the National Archives.
I hold the records of America's federal government.
They include documents, photos, maps, films, and more!

Some of my most famous records are:

- The Declaration of Independence
- The U.S. Constitution
- The Bill of Rights

Visitors can view famous documents protected in special cases.

National Zoo

I am the National Zoo!
If you like animals, you will love to visit me!
I am home to about 1,800 animals.

Some are tall, like elephants and zebras.
Some are fast, like leopards and cheetahs.
Some fly, like owls and flamingoes.
Some crawl, like alligators and snakes.

I am a giant panda.
I came to the National Zoo
from China!

National Air &
Space Museum
EASTERN
AIR LINES
344
5-AT TRI-MOTOR
FC-2

Washington, D.C., is home
to many amazing museums!

If you like airplanes, you will love
the National Air and Space Museum!
It holds the world's largest collection
of aircraft and spacecraft.

Gliders **Rockets** **Spacesuits**

Jetliners **Spacecraft** **And More!**

MUSEUM

National Museum of Natural History

MUSEUM

Do you like dinosaurs?
Do you think mummies are cool?
Do you love creepy, crawly bugs?

If you said YES, you need to visit
the National Museum of Natural History!

There's much more to see
in this very cool place.
It's likely to put
a big smile on your face!

National Museum of American History

I am the National Museum of American History!
What can you find here?
Pieces of American history from A to Z!

Here are a few examples:

- The Star-Spangled Banner flag
- Dorothy's ruby slippers from *The Wizard of Oz*
- President Lincoln's top hat

MUSEUM

SPY MUSEUM
International Spy Museum
Bureau of Engraving and Printing
Cherry Blossom Festival
Professional Sports
Washington, D.C.

There is much more to do in Washington, D.C.!

Museums and parks
Theaters and shops
Sports teams and tours
The fun never stops!

GLOSSARY

archives: a collection of historical documents or records

civil rights: the rights every person should have

district: area set aside by a government for official business

federal: relating to a nation formed by the union of several states

memorial: something preserving the memory of a person or event

monument: a structure made to preserve the memory of a person or event

obelisk: a four-sided pillar that narrows at the top, ending in a pyramid

sculptor: an artist who creates objects using materials like clay or stone